"I felt the author did a great job pulling the reader into the story. I felt like I was actually *in* the story."

–Patti Pierce, author of
Truth and Grace Homeschool Academy blog

". . .a fun read which kept us turning pages, imagining what it may have been like during Noah's time and remembering that things change, but God doesn't, and we should always be thankful. I would definitely recommend the story to those looking for clean reading for kids and Biblical fiction!"

–Martianne Stanger, author of
Training Happy Hearts blog

"This one is a page-turner. Once you start, you won't want to put it down. The writing fills your imagination with vivid imagery. One thing that was fun for us to discuss, after everyone had a turn with the book, was how the [story] aligned with the Bible."

–Crystal Heft, author of *Living Abundantly* blog

". . .a great book and we loved reading it aloud together! I recommend grabbing a copy for your own family to read!"

–Felicia Mollohan, author of *Homeschool4Life* blog

IMAGINE

The Miracles of Jesus

Matt
Koceich

BARBOUR BOOKS
An Imprint of Barbour Publishing, Inc.

Cover illustration: Simon Mendez

Published by Barbour Books, an imprint of Barbour Publishing, Inc., 1810 Barbour Drive, Uhrichsville, Ohio 44683, www.barbourbooks.com

Our mission is to inspire the world with the life-changing message of the Bible.

Member of the
Evangelical Christian
Publishers Association

Printed in the United States of America.
06693   0919   BP

THOUSANDS OF YEARS AGO

No light. No sound. . .except for the beat of his heart.

He had no idea where he was. He only knew his name.

John Le.

He couldn't remember what had happened to make the lights go out.

He reached into the nothingness with both hands, like a blind man trying to find his way across an unknown landscape. His brain tried to focus on the current situation.

Darkness smothered him and wouldn't let go.

He had a faraway thought that what was happening was all his fault.

No matter what direction he shuffled, he couldn't find a way out.

That's when his hands hit a jagged wall. It was damp and felt like dirt.

The cave!

A tiny fragment of the mystery had been solved.

I was running away from the dragon.

I couldn't go any farther.

The cave called to me.

But no one had come to save him. The end of all

things was the dark, cold cave.

No light. No joy. Just. . .nothing.

He was mad at himself for his bad decision. He should never have run into the cave.

For all those miles across the unforgiving desert, he outwitted the enemy. From the northern edge of the sea, all the way down the big river, he had run hard, staying one step ahead of the evil one.

Exhausted and mentally drained from all the wonders and signs he had witnessed, John needed to rest. The cave in the town of Bethany called to him like a powerful lighthouse beam that beckons lost souls in a storm—a strong light that reaches through the tempest and shines on the needy.

The cave called to his tired, frightened body and offered rest.

In fact, the cave offered him hope. If he could hide from the hideous beast that had followed him since this whole crazy trip started, then surely John would figure out a new plan.

There in the heart of the earth, he shuffled and followed the cave wall in an unknown direction. John prayed to see even a dab of light, but only the darkness remained.

God, please get me out of this!

Finally, a single point of light appeared on the horizon. John wasted no time and headed for it. Along the way, his feet hit things that felt like rocks and pebbles and even something quite large, but softer than stone.

The light never got bigger, but John got weaker.

God didn't seem to be listening.

And John got more disoriented.

Anxiety wrapped its misty arms around him and yanked him deeper into the hole. Sweat dripped down his face, and precious air was getting hard to find.

"Lord, if You had been here, my brother would not have died!"

He heard the person's voice—a woman's voice—just as clearly as if she were in the cave.

"Hello?"

No answer.

"Hello? Who's there?"

Still no reply.

John felt paralyzed. He had been managing the darkness without letting fear win. But the voice that talked about someone dying caused him to panic.

Why did the town of Bethany seem familiar?

Who died in Bethany?

Lazarus.

Was John in the same cave as Lazarus?

Something quite large, but softer than stone. . .

A body?

If that's really the case, I'm in here with a dead man!

No. No. No!

John ran.

Straight into a wall.

And ran again.

Into another wall.

He tripped over unseen obstacles.

So hard to breathe.

John panicked.

Instead of escaping, he went farther and farther into darkness.

After what felt like an eternity, John gave up. Trying to escape the nothingness didn't work.

He collapsed onto the damp earth.

The cave had now become his tomb. It wouldn't be long before he too became a part of the void.

God, why don't You help me?

CHAPTER 1

PRESENT DAY

LAS VEGAS, NEVADA

Sketching the lotus brought him peace.

Creating the delicate petals of the exotic flower calmed his heart.

He thought of the backpack by his feet loaded with the entire Narnia series, just waiting to be read. His sister, Marie, gifted them to him as an early birthday present. Twelve-year-old John Le loved to read.

But he was overwhelmed with the desire to make this drawing for his mom instead.

Besides, his plane was about to land, and then it would be back to reality. Back to his father and all the stress that came with being the only child in the Le home.

John was thankful that his grandmother had taught him how to draw. She told him a long time ago that making pictures with a pencil gave life to what imagination created. He missed her infectious smile every time she looked at his sketches. No matter how good or bad they were, Hoa always smiled and told him his art was wonderful.

"Cool flower."

John looked up from his art and saw a kind-looking flight attendant staring down at him. "Thanks."

"Lotus?"

John nodded. He didn't want to talk. He really wanted to finish this picture before they landed.

"Well, I think you are very talented, young man."

The plane rattled, and the attendant grabbed on to the empty seat next to John.

"The pilot says we're going through some pretty bad storms."

Tell me about it. "Do you trust the pilot in this weather?"

The attendant smiled. "Very unique question. But yes, I trust him. He's been doing this a long time."

The lady didn't leave. She just stood there and held on to the seat. John tried to ignore her as he navigated the pencil back and forth over the paper where a new lotus petal came to life.

"Did someone teach you how to draw that?"

"My grandma Hoa. She loved comparing the lotus to Jesus."

"Cool. What did she say?"

The plane shook like some giant hand had grabbed it and rocked it back and forth.

Even the plane knows what I'm heading back to. Stress. Stress. And more stress.

"Grandma always said that just like Jesus leaving His glorious throne to be born in a cold manger, the beautiful lotus starts off in the muck and darkness of a pond bottom."

"Oh, that's awesome. I like your grandma. May I sit beside you for a minute?"

Even though John wanted to finish his drawing, he didn't want the lady to fall over in the aisle.

"Okay."

"Thank you. I'm Margaret."

"I'm John."

"Hi, John. It's really nice to meet you."

Another jolt of turbulence shook the plane. A shout came from somewhere behind them; then the speaker above John's head crackled.

"This is Captain Stewart. We're in the middle of a pretty big storm cell. Please remain seated with your seat belts fastened. We should be touching down at

McCarran in about twenty minutes. Thank you."

"Wow, this one's pretty bad. At least it'll be over soon." Margaret kept her eyes on John's drawing.

Despite the storm, John kept his pencil moving. He needed to finish the lotus so he could surprise his mother. She really needed something to put a smile on her face. Anytime things got bad at home, John would sketch a lotus and give it to his mother. It was their secret code to remember Jesus.

"I think your mom is really going to like that."

I hope.

The plane rattled again, but John kept the pencil on the petal he was shading.

"John, you mentioned Jesus earlier. I want you to know He understands exactly what you're going through."

John stopped drawing and looked at the flight attendant.

"I believe in Him, but I don't think He knows what I'm going through." John looked back at the lotus flower. "If He did, why would He let bad things happen?"

Margaret turned in her seat to look John in the eyes. She put a comforting hand on his left arm.

"Look at me, John."

Eventually, John looked back up at her.

"Jesus knows your mom is devastated because she trusted your dad. Jesus also knows your dad is a mess because he trusted the casinos to answer his prayers instead of God. Jesus knows that your dad is taking his problems out on you."

How did this stranger know these things?

"Who are you? How do you know all those things about me?"

The plane rattled again.

It dropped and shot John's stomach into a spin.

No more.

God, why have You left me like this?

Why can't You protect me from all the bad things happening?

Why can't You make all this stop?

It was all too much.

John dropped the pencil on the seat-back tray.

The plane dropped again. He heard another voice from somewhere in the back yelling about the turbulence.

John couldn't breathe. His fingers began to tingle. He shut his eyes and put his hands over his face.

"John," Margaret said. "Let me help you."

"Leave me alone!" John unbuckled his seat belt and pushed his way past the flight attendant.

The plane buckled beneath his feet and caused him to stumble in the aisle. He had to make it to the bathroom. It was the only space on the entire plane where he could lock the door and be by himself. . .and his thoughts.

God, what's happening?

This is freaking me out!

Another wave of panic washed over John. The passengers stared at him with faces that reminded him of the emoticon characters in the movie *Inside Out*.

The people who wore glasses became Sadness. John saw their eyes wide open and their hands clasped together. They seemed to sing the same silent chorus. *Help us!*

The sharp-dressed ones were Fear. They all appeared to have maroon bow ties, and their faces morphed into purple blobs with big eyes.

John caught himself on an armrest as the plane dipped and rose under his feet. Flashes of lightning lit up the tiny windows while the rain continued to pour.

More loud voices.

A man with red hair yelled at John to sit down. His open mouth and red face made him Anger.

A lady wearing a green shirt and a lavender scarf looked at John like he was an alien. Disgust.

Joy was nowhere to be found.

John pushed his way down the aisle and made it to the restroom. The plane felt like it was spinning in circles.

He opened the narrow door and stepped into the tiny room. It was hard to concentrate. Where was the door lock?

John turned and found the silver knob. He slid it to the right and switched the VACANT sign to OCCUPIED.

His head hurt.

The plane spun.

John sat down on the toilet.

He noticed a piece of lined notebook paper resting on the tiny sink.

John snatched it up and read the blue, handwritten ink:

3L3CTUS

John Le

What was 3-L-3-C-T-U-S?

And who knew his name?

The plane dropped.

John let go of the paper and covered his face with his hands.

He shut his eyes, hoping it would all go away.

Sweat gathered on his skin.

Lord, I'm losing my mind!

"Open his eyes."

It sounded just like Margaret's voice. It was clear, like she was in the lavatory with him, even though she wasn't.

Please make this stop!

John let go of his sweaty face.

He opened his eyes.

CHAPTER 2

SEA OF GALILEE

A.D. 33

What in the world was happening?

The airplane had disappeared.

John was sitting, not on an airplane toilet seat, but on a wide wooden bench.

Not thousands of feet in the air, but in the middle of a group of scraggly looking men.

On a boat.

On the water.

"Friends, haven't you any fish?"

The question was not asked by any of the men on the boat. The voice came over the breeze, from somewhere in the distance.

From the low position of the sun, John guessed it was either very early morning or almost night.

"Look!" One of the bearded men stood up and

pointed at something in the distance.

John looked in the direction the man was pointing and saw the shape of a person.

Another man on the boat spoke up. "Who is this who asks about our catch?"

"I don't know. But I can't believe it. All night on the sea and not a single fish."

The man standing said, "Nathanael, please believe that we will catch fish tomorrow. You've been carrying a lot of things in your heart. I know that God will not forget us."

"You're right, Didymus. I'm sorry. That was just so much work for nothing," Nathanael replied.

John rubbed his face. How on earth did he get on a primitive fishing boat with a bunch of dirty fishermen? Where did the airplane go? Where was Margaret?

Then, in unison, the fishermen answered the person who asked about catching fish. "NO!"

John was confused.

The shape in the distance became a man standing on the shore where the water lapped up over the land.

"Throw your net on the right side of the boat, and you will find some."

John watched the men who surrounded him reach

down and grab a heavy fishing net. Together, they obeyed the command and tossed it over the right side. John watched it sink below the surface.

After a few minutes of silence, the men tried hauling the net in but couldn't.

"It's filled with fish!"

"Impossible!"

At that moment, a connection was made. John remembered what all this was. The Bible story where Jesus returned from the grave and appeared to His friends by the Sea of Galilee! How on earth was he able to be in the middle of this miracle?

"It is the Lord!"

One of the fishermen, who stood in front of John, wrapped his outer garment around him. The man smiled and jumped over the side of the boat into the water.

"Simon Peter!" another man yelled after the one who jumped in.

John watched Simon Peter swim toward the shore.

"Let's go. We are about a hundred yards away. Since the net is too heavy, we can pull it in to shore."

The fishermen lowered two big wooden oars into the water and started rowing.

When they reached the shore, John hopped out of the boat and landed on the sand. He wiped his hands off on his jeans and looked over at the man who had asked if the men had caught any fish.

John knew the story. That meant the robed man with long hair and an epic beard standing in front of him was... Jesus!

No. Way.

Simon Peter crawled out of the water and ran to Jesus and gave him a huge bear hug.

Behind Jesus, John noticed a fire made from burning coals. On it, fish were cooking.

After hugging Peter, Jesus said, "Bring some of the fish you have just caught."

John watched Peter climb back into the boat and grab the net. The disciple climbed back into the shallow water and dragged the net ashore.

The other disciples scurried around the open net and began counting the large fish that were in it.

John kept staring at Jesus.

Am I dead?

"No, you're not dead!" Jesus turned and looked directly at John.

John was so excited and freaked out at the same

time, he couldn't talk. He was standing in front of Jesus!

His body felt electric, like the time his grandparents took him on the X-Scream ride 866 feet above Vegas on top of the Stratosphere tower. The buzz of excitement came on the elevator ride up, as John thought about the thrill of being strapped in a tiny car and being dangled out over the edge.

John's life up to this point had been the elevator ride up the tower. He thought it would be cool to see Jesus and could only wonder what that would actually be like. And there were plenty of days when he wished he could just give Jesus a hug and feel all of life's stress simply wash away.

But then came the freaked-out part. Belted in the roller coaster and being tilted back and forth so far up in the sky. John's body revolted and wanted out, but that couldn't happen until the ride ended.

Standing on the shore of the actual Sea of Galilee, in front of Jesus. . .

John was certifiably freaked out!

"I love you so much, John. Don't be afraid."

"Jesus?"

"Yes, precious child." Jesus spread His arms open.

John stepped closer and opened his arms too.

He closed his eyes and got the hug of a hundred million lifetimes!

Safe.

Warm.

Eternal.

"I am so glad you're here, John Le. You make Me happy."

"How is this happening?"

Jesus hugged John a second time.

Safer.

Warmer.

Eternal.

"I love you, John Le. I want you to see and feel just how special I made you."

One of the disciples shouted, "We've counted a hundred and fifty-three fish. And, we've checked the net and it is not torn!"

Jesus smiled again at John.

"Come, friends, and have breakfast with Me."

John stood with his mouth open, not able to believe that he was standing next to Jesus! He watched Him take the bread and rip chunks off for each of His friends. Then He did the same thing with the fish.

I'm laughing, John. You think you're somebody important now that you're with Jesus?

It was his dad's voice. Crystal clear. Just as real as him standing on the beach having breakfast with Jesus!

John, you are not important.

Why was this beautiful moment getting wrecked by the sound of his father's voice?

"John, what's wrong, My child?"

It was Jesus.

"It's my dad's voice. I don't know why, but it's like he's right here with us."

"Dear child, your father can't hurt you here."

Of course I can. You still won't matter when you get back to reality.

"He's still talking to me." John blinked his eyes a few times.

Jesus offered him His outstretched hand. "Come, John. You've had a long day. Get some rest, and then you and I will talk about more than just your earthly father."

John couldn't concentrate. The ugly voice in his head distracted him from the beautiful moment of sharing a meal with Jesus and His friends.

"*SCREEEEEEEEEEEEEE. SCREEEEEEEEE-*

EEEEEE. SCREEEEEEEEEEEEEEEEE."

The hideous sounds came from the sky above them. It sounded like a billion ear-piercing school fire alarms going off at the same time.

John looked up and screamed.

CHAPTER 3

Far up in the sky, where beautiful white clouds floated across a sea of endless blue, it wailed again.

An enormous red dragon that looked like a war machine used its monstrous spiked tail to sweep stars out of the heavens. They shot to the earth and landed on scorched ground. Each star transformed into a human shape.

The dragon landed in the middle of the sea, pushing a massive circle of water up like a bomb had gone off underground. All around the lake, black streaks zoomed down from the sky and collided with the earth.

John couldn't believe what his eyes were seeing.

The hideous red beast emerged from the sea and flung its horn-covered head around, looking for something.

John, it's me. You don't really matter.

It was his dad's voice again.

The dragon's head stopped moving. It stared right at John!

Out of the corner of his eye, John noticed that the ribbons of black that had crashed to the earth were now rising all around the shore. They looked like soldiers.

John, things are not going to change. You've never been important and you never will be.

John turned to run, but not before he saw the dragon breathe an explosion of fire, the flames reaching out to John across the surface of the sea. A wave of burning air washed over him.

In unison, the black-clad military men started running toward John.

He looked around for Jesus and the fishermen but couldn't see them.

They were just there eating breakfast, and now they were gone.

I told you, John, it's me. Go ahead and run, but I will teach you a lesson.

The dragon talked to John in his father's voice.

You don't matter, John.

The creature rose up out of the water and flapped its massive wings.

In fact, your faith is so weak, you really are a disappointment to God.

Another strong pump of its wings, and the dragon shot back up into the sky.

The soldiers were much closer now.

It looked like they were all carrying heavy chains.

John saw a cave at the top of a nearby hill. That was his only chance at survival.

He broke into a sprint.

The dragon switched directions and began gliding back down...

...toward the cave!

The soldiers were swinging the chains over their heads like rodeo cowboys preparing to lasso a calf.

John stopped.

The dragon landed on the side of the hill, right in front of the cave entrance.

John, there's nowhere to hide.

The soldiers closed in from the sea. Their uniforms were more like black jeans and black hoodies.

The dragon was right. There was nowhere to hide.

Up to the dragon or down to the soldiers.

John decided that he would not just stand there and let these crazy things get him.

No, he was going to try and put his faith to the test.

"Jesus, please help me!"

John felt his fear of what his eyes saw wane long enough for him to realize there was nothing to either his right or left except empty hillside.

He took off running to his left.

The soldiers changed direction and followed him.

"Jesus!" John yelled out as he ran. "You just gave Your friends all that fish. Please, I need a miracle to get away from these things!"

The dragon wailed and spit more fire into the sky in angry protest.

JOHN! THIS IS FOOLISH! YOU ARE JUST A BOY! YOU DON'T MATTER!

His father's voice rang out and caused John to cringe. He closed his eyes and tripped over a large stone. John went tumbling to the ground, scraping his hands along the ground as he used them for brakes.

The dragon soared in a circle for the longest time, like a hawk assessing its prey.

After a while, the enormous beast landed in the valley, no more than a hundred yards away.

All of that running for nothing, John.

"Jesus, please. . ."

Before John could finish his plea for help, a tremendous burst of light followed by a loud bang erupted from somewhere in the sky behind the dragon, causing the great beast to turn its head.

The soldiers also turned as one big angry mob to see what caused the new explosion.

John's mind was blown away by what came next.

All around him, across the entire valley, stood horses, and on the horses sat glorious, shining people. There were also carts with wheels drawn by other horses. The glowing people stood on the carts, all holding swords of fire!

There was a loud yell of angry voices, from which army John couldn't tell.

Soldiers who followed the dragon raised their chains and started running toward John.

The dragon shot another blast of fire from its mouth. It flung its tail around in a powerful swirl of red monstrous flesh.

The shining people spurred their horses and drove their chariots to intercept the horde that was closing in on John.

The dragon's soldiers lifted their chains and swung

them in John's direction, but the army of light swung their flaming swords and cut the chains.

Balls of fire from the clash splattered out over the dragon's army.

Screams filled the air.

Another wave of horsemen took off after the dragon.

The creature shot out more fire in defense.

JOHN, I WILL GET YOU!

The horsemen poured over the dragon like a tidal wave of radiant light.

One of the shining people broke away from the attack to approach John. He got down from the horse he'd been riding on.

"Are you all right, child?"

John looked at his hands like they were the health indicator for the rest of his body. "I think so."

"My name is Michael. I'm here to help you."

"What are you? An angel?"

"Yes, but it's getting late, and you need your rest."

Before John could ask any questions, the angel disappeared.

In a blink of an eye, all the armies and dragon were gone.

John found a small spot where the tall grass had been trampled during the skirmish. He lay down and closed his eyes.

Sleep grabbed hold of him quickly and took him to a place where dreams were outlawed and nothingness waited.

CHAPTER 4

John opened his eyes.

The tall grass swayed around him. The sun was up, so he must have gotten a good sleep. It took him a minute to remember where he was. He thought he'd had the craziest dream about being chased by a talking dragon and dudes in black clothes.

And the dragon sounded like his dad.

And he was saved by guys that looked like they had rays of light shooting from their skin!

Something stirred in his young brain that reminded him it hadn't been a dream. John jumped up to check if there were any more dragons or scary, chain-wielding bad guys. There was nothing. Just the empty valley running down to the sea.

John started walking back toward the water, hoping to find Jesus.

After a few minutes, his attention was taken by a white bird flying peacefully by. It looked like a dove, and the beautiful creature flew away from the sea. It was heading in the direction of the sun, which was now a big fireball in the western sky.

John didn't know why, but he kept following the white bird.

As he walked, John noticed a man who was riding a horse a little farther down the path. The man was covered in a bright red robe that had huge sleeves and gold trim. The fabric was shiny and covered the man from shoulders to feet. It looked as if the man had a white robe on underneath the red one. He wore a headdress of red with a thick band of gold around the rim.

John hurried to catch up.

"Excuse me!"

The man didn't turn around but instead kept guiding the horse.

"I don't mean to bother you, but I'm lost."

The stranger still didn't make eye contact with John. "My son's dying! I have to find the man called Jesus."

"That's who I'm looking for too!"

John jogged a little to catch up to the man and then kept pace with his horse.

"I am so sorry to hear about your son."

John thought about the miracles that Jesus did. In this place, John wasn't seeing them in order, but that didn't matter to him. He was getting to be right in the middle of them!

He sorted through his Bible knowledge and thought about a miracle where Jesus healed a man's dying son.

John said, "Are you a royal official?"

"Yes. I work for King Herod. How did you know? Who are you?"

John thought about what to say to the man. "Your son is going to be okay!"

The man finally stopped the horse and turned to look down at John. "What kind of clothes are you wearing? And how do you know my son? Who are you?"

"My name is John Le. I don't know how on earth I got here, but I live in a place called Nevada. I go to church and read this book called the Bible. And in the Bible, it says that your son lives!"

"You can't know such things! Leave me be. I have to find Jesus."

John wanted to be respectful. He couldn't imagine the pain and desperation the man was feeling. But he had to keep up with him because that would eventually get him back to Jesus.

"I really am sorry that your son is hurting. I will pray for him."

The official snapped the reins and made the horse resume walking. "Are you a prophet?"

"No, sir. I'm just a normal kid from Las Vegas."

"I've come from Capernaum. Sixteen miles away. I need to find Jesus. I hear He is in Cana."

"Can I please ride with you?"

The man pulled up on the reins. "Whoa!"

The horse stopped.

"Please? I need to find Jesus too."

The official considered John. He reached down and pulled him up onto the horse.

"Thank you!"

After a long time of riding over the dirt path, the official spoke. "We have reached Cana. We will not stop until we find the only One who can heal my son."

"Yes, sir." John felt part of a team.

It didn't take long to find Jesus. Everyone was still talking about the man who had performed a miracle at a wedding in their village three years before.

When they followed the directions of an elderly woman, they got to a part of town that looked like an outdoor market. John scanned the large crowd and saw Jesus standing in the middle.

"There He is!"

The official helped John get down off the horse. Then the official jumped down.

They both threaded their way through the gathering.

John felt his body fill with an electric love the closer he got to Jesus.

Jesus! I can't believe I'm standing here with Jesus!

The official pushed past the last few people and made his way to the front of the crowd. He kneeled down and pleaded, "Please, Jesus. Please come and heal my son. He is sick and close to death!"

Jesus looked at the man and then over at John. Then to everyone in the crowd, He said, "Unless you people see signs and wonders, you will never believe."

John felt the words flow *through* his body like they were some kind of invisible substance. They caused him to think about his dad. *I am protecting you from your father. You have to believe this even though you don't feel it.*

The official spoke. His plea for mercy brought John back to the moment.

"Sir, come back to Capernaum with me before my child dies."

Jesus looked at the man. "Go. Your son will live."

John watched the man nod and get up to leave.

The official said, "I trust You!" He made his way back through the crowd.

Even though John knew the story, it was different being in it. John expected the man to beg Jesus to come back to Capernaum so He could go and heal his son. Instead, he just mounted his horse and prepared to leave. John thought about how the man had traveled all those hours and miles to save his son. And now, the man simply believed that Jesus was going to do what He said He was going to do.

John watched the official gallop away, back in the direction they had come. He looked at Jesus. "You just healed his son, didn't You?"

"Yes, child. When he gets close to home, his servants are going to meet him on the road and tell him that his son is alive."

John smiled. Here he was getting to talk to Jesus! He didn't want this to end.

Jesus put his hands on John's shoulders. "I know you are worried about your dad. It will be all right."

John told Jesus about the dragon and the soldiers.

"I know. It will be all right. Don't be afraid," Jesus said.

"I couldn't find You when all of that was happening."

"I was with you the whole time. Your being here is all about your faith journey. That means trusting Me to be strong enough to always take care of you. Trust the things that your eyes can't see just as that father trusted what he couldn't see."

John considered his Savior's words. Part of him wondered why Jesus just couldn't prevent the bad stuff from happening, but he was too embarrassed to ask.

Jesus gave John a hug and told him a second time not to worry. "I am calling you to do great things. There is an enemy that will try and stop you. He will come at you in different ways. Don't worry about anything. Say no, and trust that I am with you. Stand up, and with My power you will defeat his plans!"

John took a deep breath and exhaled.

Maybe he didn't have to worry about things. Just being here with Jesus was enough.

As soon as John had that last thought, his father's voice returned.

Son, I can't believe you.

He shook his head, hoping to shake the voice away.

It didn't work.

The voice came again.

You actually think you are something special, don't you?

John watched the people around him fade away—even Jesus.

The world lost its color.

"Jesus!"

But there wasn't a reply.

John, you aren't special. You are just a boy who makes one mistake after another.

The voice was so loud, John shut his eyes and covered his ears.

His father was screaming.

John dropped to his knees, eyes still shut. Hands over his ears.

"Jesus, please. Make this stop!"

CHAPTER 5

I'm going to remind you, John. You are not important.

His dad's voice again. Not nearly as loud this time.

John uncovered his ears and opened his eyes.

He was alone in the world that had lost its color.

There was no sign of the dragon. Or his dad. Or the dragon's soldiers.

"Jesus, I hear it again." John turned, but Jesus and the others had disappeared again, just like they had done by the sea.

He had to remember what had just happened. Yes, he had witnessed another miracle as he watched the royal official beg Jesus for mercy to heal his dying son. Then he watched the same broken rich man take Jesus at His word and ride off out of Cana.

For a minute he thought about his own dad. Would he go so far out of the way to get help for John if John was really sick? That made him think about having to return home after spending the summer with his sister.

John let fear of having to deal with his dad take over. That's when he heard the voice again.

You should be ashamed of yourself.

How could his dad get to him out here in this other land?

Then John noticed a bizarre thing. There were all these people—men, boys, girls—who suddenly appeared all over the place. Some stood in big groups, others sat in pairs, all over the prairie for as far as he could see. As John navigated the masses, he knew these were fathers with their kids. Everyone was smiling and happy. Laughing. Hugging.

Hi, John. See how these dads love their children? This is how it's supposed to be. Too bad for you. This is something you're never going to experience.

John spun around, still expecting his father to be there with that sarcastic look on his face. It was the one that John got every time something didn't go right in the Le house. If John forgot to fill the dog's dishes with food and water in the evening, the next morning would bring his dad's index finger pointed at his son's face and the look of closed lips, wide eyes, and shaking head. The expression that said, "I can't believe how less-than-everyone-else you are."

John tried to focus on the here and now. The hundreds of people all over were still enjoying each other's company. He started catching snippets of the conversations and heard a lot of people saying, "I love you." In return, John also heard "I love you so much." The dads and their kids held hands, looking at each other with compassion.

"Have you seen Jesus?" John asked a young man who stood nearby.

The young man acted like John wasn't there. The guy never looked his way.

John asked again, "Have you seen Jesus walk by here?"

The man ignored John.

John walked on to another man and his children. They were sitting on the grass.

"Excuse me. Have you guys seen Jesus?"

The man's daughter looked up and gave John an ugly look.

The man did the same.

Neither one of them said a word to John.

John spent a long time trying to find Jesus in the

crowd but came up empty. Not one person said a word to him, and most never looked at him. He felt invisible and unwanted.

You aren't loved by your dad.

John froze. In front of him, no more than twenty feet away, was a huge dark snake. The body had to be at least fifteen feet long, and it was colored olive green with black splotches all down the length of it. Neon-green eyes were set closer to the top of its head.

John, I know you can hear me.

First the dragon, and now the snake.

Look at how happy all these children and their fathers are, and not one of them has said a word to you. You don't matter to them either.

John started walking away from the snake, but the slithering serpent caught up with him and crawled over the ground only feet away. John would be killed if the snake attacked. It was like one of those anacondas he'd seen on the science channel.

John, you are wasting time.

"Leave me alone," John told the snake. John switched directions, hoping to get far away from it.

The reptile's long tongue flicked the air in front of its big, blocky head. It also switched its course, no doubt so it could stay close.

John kept an eye out for Jesus, but he couldn't find Him anywhere.

The crowds of people acted like they couldn't see the massive snake.

I'm never leaving you alone. Ever.

John figured the snake would have already attacked him if that was the creature's ultimate desire. Since John was still alive, he decided to test his theory.

John ran through the crowd and found a man with his children who were sitting on brightly colored blankets. The children were all different ages and sizes. He sat down in the middle of the group and waited for the snake to come.

John tried thinking about how he was back in the time of the Bible stories. But he kept getting distracted by the snake. It was closer now. So close, yet none of the people around John seemed to notice. They were all lost in each other. . .smiling, talking, laughing.

John, they are important to each other. Too bad you don't know what that feels like.

When the snake made its way to where he was sitting, John asked, "Why are you following me?"

I told you, John. You need a reminder that you don't

matter to your father. But you matter to me.

Something wasn't right. John heard words he wanted to hear from his father—words that sounded good—but something didn't feel right.

The people that were sitting around John got up and walked away from him. In fact, all the groups that were anywhere close by did the same.

Only one girl in the crowd stopped and looked at John. She seemed to be close in age to him. "You should leave."

See, they all ignored you, and then the one who actually said something told you to get out.

"I am not going to listen to you."

You're not important to anyone else. No one else cares about you.

The snake kept its distance.

"Jesus, if You're here, please help me!"

John, you don't matter to Jesus.

"Jesus, I need You!"

The snake recoiled. Its massive form was slow to retreat.

Come on. You don't think Jesus is going to help, do you?

"JESUS!"

At that exact second, the snake exploded into a

million tiny particles and blew away on the wind.

John fell to his knees. He slammed both hands on the ground in front of him.

Finally, he let the tears come that had been building up like water held behind a dam.

CHAPTER 6

The pieces of ashy snake blew away on the wind until no trace of the ugly creature remained. John had said the name *Jesus*, and the snake blew up. There was power in that name, and he'd just witnessed that power. *Amazing.*

He still couldn't figure out how all of this was happening.

One minute he was on the plane flying back home, the next minute he was sitting on an ancient wooden fishing boat with the disciples.

And then eating breakfast with Jesus!

He couldn't believe it.

As the last reptile flake floated far away and disappeared, John noticed that the normal colors of the world quickly returned.

Blue sky.

Green grass.

White clouds.

Yellow sun.

It was amazing compared to the bleak land he had just seen.

John looked around for Jesus, but he was still alone. The crowds of people had all gone away.

He noticed that there was a well-worn path close by that led up and over a hill. John decided to follow it and see where it led.

He traveled quite some distance before he finally saw another person. It looked like an older man who was walking slowly. John ran up to him and introduced himself.

"Hi. I'm John."

"Hi, John. I'm Simon."

"Where are you going?"

"To Jerusalem for the festival."

Jerusalem?

John had an idea. "Do you know Jesus?"

The stranger said, "I've heard of the man but have never seen Him in person."

John knew that Jesus spent a lot of time in Jerusalem. "Ask around when you get to the city. You just have to meet Jesus! Your life will never be the same."

"Okay, young man. That sounds good. I will keep my eyes open for this Jesus."

John thanked the man and walked on ahead of him. The land of grass and hills stayed the same.

After a while, John was glad to see more people ahead of him on the path. They weren't dressed like modern people but instead wore cream robes and fabric wrapped around their heads. He caught up to them and followed, hoping they would lead him the rest of the way to the city.

John felt confident that he would find Jesus there.

At some point the landscape changed. Far ahead, a huge stone city spread out before them. It was beautiful. Like a floating fortress. . .

Someone in the group called out, "Jerusalem!"

John saw a rectangular castle-looking building that had four towers. He asked one of the travelers about it.

"That is the Antonia Fortress. Herod built it. It's the headquarters of the Roman soldiers. They have six hundred soldiers stationed there to keep order in the temple courts."

John still couldn't believe that he was getting to see

all this! Ancient Jerusalem. *Unbelievable!*

He followed the crowd as they walked up to the impressive walls of the city and then through an opening.

"This is called the Sheep Gate," said one of the women. "This is the entrance that sheep and lambs are brought through to be sacrificed."

John took in the scene. They were standing under a covered walkway.

A man in the group said, "This is just north of the temple. Pilgrims who journey to our city use the pool to purify themselves before they worship."

John wasn't sure what that meant, but he made a mental note to look it up later. He did think it was interesting that Jesus was known as the Lamb who went to the cross as a sacrifice for people's sins, and they had just walked through the Sheep Gate.

They walked under the archway and into the city. John saw a huge rectangular structure. Inside there were two square swimming pools. Next to one of the pools, a lot of people were in the water, and many were also standing on the edge. Some were even sitting on the ground.

An older man with stringy white hair saw John staring at the water. He came up beside John and started talking. "That pool is called Bethesda. The word means *house of grace*. We also have a word in Aramaic, *hesda*, which means *shame, or disgrace*. The people who go into that water and get healed find grace can come from the pain they've had to deal with their whole lives. Those who can't move, who sit like beggars, are a disgrace to some who see them and wish they would leave."

John thought about what the man said. There were so many sick people in this place. People who couldn't see. People who couldn't stand. It made him think of his own father who had his own pain. To John and his mom, he was acting like a disgrace with all the gambling and anger. But to Jesus, he had a chance of finding grace and forgiveness.

All the healthy people walked by like the sick weren't there. Everybody except Jesus. He appeared at the edge of the crowd and then stopped.

"Someone, please help me. I've been sick for thirty-eight years."

The voice belonged to a man lying on the ground.

Jesus saw the man. "Would you like to be healed?"

"Sir, I have no one to put me in the pool when the water is moving. While I try to get in, another one gets in first." The sick man pleaded with Jesus for help.

The stranger who had been explaining things said, "An angel of the Lord comes at certain times and makes the water move."

John remembered that part of the story.

The man continued, "Whoever gets into the water first after the angel moves it is healed of whatever sickness he or she has."

Jesus said, "Get up! Pick up your mat and walk."

Immediately, the man was healed.

"Thank You, Jesus! Thank You, Jesus!"

He picked up his mat and walked.

John had just witnessed another miracle.

The crowd went along with their routines, most not noticing the miracle that had just taken place.

Jesus turned to John. "That man does not know who I am."

John didn't know what to say. Instead, he just followed Jesus and the others past the pools to the temple courtyard.

John's attention was taken by a scream off to his left. He looked and saw people running in every direction. A mass of chaos in the streets of Jerusalem. John looked and couldn't believe what he was seeing.

The cause of all the screaming was a lion!

Right there in the middle of the people.

An uncaged, wild beast.

But something was wrong.

This lion didn't look majestic like Aslan in the Narnia movies.

No, this lion looked wicked.

Instead of bright, clean golden fur, this lion looked dirty. Like it hadn't seen water or rain in a very long time.

And this scary creature wasn't wide and strong and regal. This lion appeared much too thin for its big frame. Lanky, like its extra-large, greasy coat had been draped over its bones with hardly any muscle in between.

That's when the lion spied John. It took a few steps in his direction and bared huge fangs that looked more blood red than white.

The roar was loud and powerful.

The lion pounced to attack.

John ran.

CHAPTER 7

John ran as fast as his legs could move. He made it down the covered archway and slipped behind one of the big stone columns. What was happening?

First the dragon.

Then the snake.

Now the lion.

John racked his brain.

Who was chasing him?

The devil?

He knew that in the book of Revelation the devil was described as a red dragon. In the Garden of Eden, he was a snake. John thought about where in the Bible the devil was described as a lion. Then it hit him. *First Peter 5:8. "Be alert and of sober mind. Your enemy the devil prowls around like a roaring lion looking for someone to devour."*

John peeked out from his hiding place and noticed

the lion had left behind patches of fire where his huge paws had touched the ground.

The lion moved closer.

John, I can't believe my own son would treat me this way.

His dad's voice again. Using the same words John heard over and over in his bedroom when his dad would discipline him.

Each time John tried to talk to his dad, his dad would tell him to be quiet and—

—that nothing he said or did mattered.

John wished it would all go away. That was one reason why he wanted to stay here in the Bible land. Facing his father was the last thing he wanted to do.

The lion, despite its mangy, weak appearance, lunged at John and slammed into the stone column that he was hiding behind, cracking it in half.

John bolted for the next column, but the supernatural cat kept the pursuit going. Again, instead of running around the column to catch John, the lion slammed into it like the first one, busting the stone into loose chunks.

John was running out of hiding places.

Colliding with two massive stone structures did nothing to stop the predator from wanting to capture its prey. It stood up on its two hind paws and looked for John.

John looked around for somewhere to escape.

He couldn't see Jesus or the disciples.

Everyone else had fled.

There was an opening on the far side of the pool building. It was his only chance.

He couldn't outrun the crazed cat, but maybe he could outswim it. It was his only shot. John jumped into the pool water. The lion did not jump in after him but stayed on the deck and watched.

John pumped his arms and legs, propelling his body across the water to the other side.

The lion started to jump in but then stopped. His big furry head looked around like it was considering a better alternative to catch its prey.

John reached the other side and pulled himself out.

The lion, despite its awkward motions, loped around the perimeter of the pool and ran up behind John.

John bolted for the doorway.

His mistake was looking back.

As John slid through the doorway, he felt fire rake across the back of his left leg.

The lion's claw felt like a thousand needles stabbing his skin.

Adrenaline helped John keep running. He got out

into the courtyard but couldn't find anywhere to hide. He spun around and saw the castle rising above the city.

That was it. If he could make it there, he could get one of the Roman soldiers to help him.

Hey, John. Did you forget about me? I told you I wasn't going away! You have to deal with me. You should have minded your own business. But no, you had to go and pray about things.

The sound of the familiar voice freaked him out. He'd forgotten that the dragon and the serpent had his dad's voice.

Now the lion did too!

Desperation kept John from worrying about the cuts on the back of his leg.

"Jesus! I need You!"

John took off toward the fortress. The whole time he looked for a way inside the imposing structure.

The nightmare with fangs followed.

"Jesus, please help me!"

This last plea to his Savior wasn't just words spoken because he didn't know what else to say. John shouted those four words in faith. Faith that Jesus was going to save him because Jesus keeps His promises.

At that exact moment a Roman soldier stepped out from a doorway at the base of the Antonia Fortress. He wielded a powerful sword in his right hand and a shield in his left.

John ran to the guard just as the lion opened his mouth to get him.

The lion pounced.

John made eye contact with the guard and then hit the ground.

The soldier rammed the blade deep into the lion's body.

That's okay, John.

I'll find another way to get you.

Just wait.

I'm coming.

CHAPTER 8

The sun was setting in the late afternoon sky. Vibrant colors painted the ancient Bible world.

John got up to thank the guard, but the guard was gone. John looked up and saw that the fortress was gone too. He looked back. The lion had vanished.

Despite the fear of almost getting mauled by a ferocious lion, John felt a warm feeling of love in his heart.

He looked around and realized all of Jerusalem had disappeared. The landscape had changed from city to grassland.

What he did see was a huge crowd of people—men, women, and children—walking behind a small group of men. They were all walking toward a large body of water.

John hurried to catch up to the crowd. When

he got closer, his heart jumped in his chest because he heard different people confirm who the small group was!

He followed the crowd back around the edge of the water to the far shore.

John could hear different voices rise above the people.

"There's Jesus! He has done great things!"

"There He is. Jesus healed my friend!"

"Oh, I hope He can help me!"

The disciples talked to each other about the huge crowd. One of them turned to Jesus.

"Send the crowd away so they can go to the surrounding villages and countryside and find food and lodging."

Jesus said, "You give them something to eat."

The landscape changed and started getting steeper the farther they walked. Finally, Jesus stopped and had John and the disciples sit.

"Philip," Jesus said.

"Yes, Jesus."

Jesus motioned to the crowd coming toward them. "Where shall we buy bread for these people to eat?"

Philip looked nervous. "It would take more than half

a year's wages to buy enough bread for each one to have a bite!"

John saw another disciple stand up. He remembered it was Andrew, Simon Peter's brother. Andrew walked over and stood by a young boy who was at the front of the crowd. "Teacher, here is a boy with five small barley loaves and two small fish, but how far will they go among so many?"

John flashed back to running away from the lion. At first, he couldn't focus on anything but how he could survive the attack. He'd forgotten about how Jesus said not to be afraid. He had let fear take over. Now the disciples were doing it. They were locked into what their eyes could see instead of remembering the invisible power of Jesus.

"Have them sit down in groups of about fifty each."

The mountainside was beautiful. Grass flowed as far as John could see.

John heard someone from the crowd say, "There are so many of us, Jesus. We will sit, but how can You feed us all?"

The disciples started telling the people to sit in groups of fifty. John joined in and walked through the humongous crowd, instructing them to sit. It took forever, but eventually everyone was sitting down in groups on the grass.

John looked at the boy holding the bread and fish. "Hello."

The boy waved.

John looked at the massive crowd and then back at the small amount of food the boy was holding. "Do you really believe that what you're holding can feed all of these people?"

The boy smiled. "I believe that Jesus can feed them."

John had no comeback. He let the boy's words sink in.

"I also believe that the disciples have a hard time believing. They act out of fear instead of trust. They look at what the world can see, but miss the power of Yeshua."

The power of Jesus.

Believe. . .in the power of Jesus.

The boy smiled again. "Can I tell you something else?"

John nodded. "Sure."

"The dragon, snake, and lion. Think about how you beat them."

"How do you know about them?" John couldn't believe this kid knew what had happened to him.

"They tried to get me too."

John closed his eyes. He took a deep breath and opened them again. "I called out to Jesus for help."

The boy smiled a third time. "Yes, you were at a point where Jesus was all you had. That's when your faith was at its strongest. Remember that. It's all about faith."

John tried to process what the boy just told him.

Jesus took the five small loaves of bread and gave thanks. John watched as Jesus directed the disciples to hand out the food. They started handing out pieces of bread to all those who were seated. Not only did they not run out of bread, but they gave each person as much as they wanted!

How did they do that? John was watching them tear off chunks of bread, but somehow, miraculously, the bread never went away. It was just there and didn't get used up. The crowd was grabbing the food like they hadn't eaten in months. But still, the bread remained.

Then Jesus took the two fish and held them up to the sky. "Thank You, Father, for this food. Thank You for meeting our needs. May Your will be done now and forever."

And just like before, the disciples started feeding the crowd. John watched as they tore off pieces of the fish and served the groups. Each person ate as much as they wanted, and the fish never ran out!

It was dark by the time all the people had finished eating.

Jesus said, "Gather the pieces that are left over. Let nothing be wasted."

John grabbed a basket and started gathering pieces of the leftover barley loaves. When his basket was full, he brought it back to where Jesus was standing. Eleven more baskets filled completely with bread were also brought to the front by the disciples.

Not only were the people fed, but there were twelve baskets filled with leftovers!

John understood that when Jesus blesses, it is in a way that blows away human understanding.

The crowd started to get to their feet.

"Surely this is the Prophet who is come into the world!" The crowd started chanting this over and over. John felt like he was on the stage of a rock concert.

"He needs to be our king!"

"Let's get Him and make Him our king!"

"Yes! Jesus will be our new leader!"

Jesus slipped away from the crowd and His other friends.

John watched Jesus withdraw to another mountain by Himself.

He started to follow but stopped when he noticed a new person standing by the water. He was dressed in jeans and a red-and-navy-plaid shirt. He waved at John. John ran down to talk to him.

CHAPTER 9

"Are you from Las Vegas?"

"Dallas."

"How did you get here?"

The man looked at John. "I have no idea! I was flying to Kansas on a business trip and there was turbulence. I went to the bathroom and closed my eyes. It was scary!"

John couldn't believe it. What were the odds that this guy who was from his same time would be here? "Me too!"

"Really?"

"Yes!" John relayed all that had happened to him since landing here. "Jesus is here!"

The man nodded but didn't have the reaction John was thinking he would have. Instead, the guy changed the subject.

"I think I might know how to get back."

John was confused. He hadn't thought about going back. He didn't really want to go back and give up being able to see and hug Jesus!

"Really?"

"I think so. But forgive me, I forgot my social skills. My name is Nate L. Davis." The man stuck out his left hand to shake. Odd.

"Hi. I'm John. John Le."

"Come on, John, let me show you how we might be able to get back."

John looked around. He couldn't see Jesus or the disciples. Something wasn't sitting right with John. Something about this guy was off.

The dragon.

The snake.

The lion.

But there was nothing here. Just a man named Nate L. Davis who had a possible way of getting home.

Still, something didn't feel right.

"No, I'm going to find Jesus."

"Suit yourself, but right over here I saw an opening."

John stopped. Caution raised another flag. "Then how come you didn't go through it?"

"Because I saw you and thought you might need help getting back."

That made sense. Maybe it wouldn't hurt to follow the guy. John decided he would keep his distance, and if anything funny happened, he'd take off running.

"Okay, let's go."

"Great. Come on." The man led John to a place on the shore where there was a fallen tree trunk, half in the shallow water, half resting on the sand.

"Now, sit on the trunk and look at the water."

John sat on the fallen tree and pulled his knees up to his chin.

"That's it. Now look out at the horizon."

John would normally think this was ridiculous, but back here in the ancient world it seemed like anything was possible.

"I don't see anything."

"Just wait."

John kept staring out at the horizon. After a minute the scene did change. The water went away, and he was sitting in front of his house back in Vegas. A lady that looked like his mother was standing there. She saw him.

"John?"

"Mom?"

"Yes, Johnny. Where have you been? And why are you sitting in the yard? Come on in before you get sick."

John got up. He knew something was wrong. His mother had never, not once in his whole life, called him Johnny. John saw Nate standing there in the street behind him. "Go on. You're home. Go."

Jesus said there was still work to be done.

Nate stepped closer to John. "You are home, John. Why aren't you going to your mother?"

John tried to figure out a way to get away from this crazy guy.

"Come on, John," the lady he knew wasn't his mother called again from the porch.

"Help me, Lord."

John turned around and walked back to the street.

To Nate he said, "No! I will not listen to you! Jesus is calling me to do a great thing. You will not stop me. Jesus said I need to trust Him. I'm learning that now. I will trust even if my eyes can't see Him. There's still more for me to see, so I'm going back."

"You're crazy."

"I am going to follow Jesus."

Nate shook his head.

When John got to the middle of the street, his home disappeared and was replaced by the Bible land. He was back sitting on the fallen tree at the edge of the sea.

Nate was standing on the shore, not too far away.

John said, "What was that all about?"

"John, I was trying to help you get out of here. I can't believe you walked away from your mom like that."

John was now able to see that Nate was lying.

He wished he could find Jesus.

"John, if you don't want to go home, at least let me help you talk to your dad."

How did this guy know anything about his dad?

"That's okay. I'm just going to look for Jesus." John started walking away from Nate.

"What if I told you I know your dad and he will listen to me? What if I told you that if I talk to him he will never be mean to you or your mother again?"

That sounded great. But no, this guy was a liar.

John just wanted to find Jesus.

Nate stepped a little closer to him. "We'll get him out here and have a chat. He will be overwhelmed at what he sees here. That's when I'll remind him of his mistakes and let him know how he needs to act in the future."

Again, it sounded great, but John didn't want to deal with a liar. He had to find Jesus.

"Okay, so you don't want to talk. I get it. Just watch, then." Nate stepped on the fallen tree and looked out toward the horizon. John watched like he was an audience member at a magic show and Nate was the magician. He really was curious to see how Nate could get his dad here.

Nate stretched his hands out.

Nothing happened.

John didn't know what the guy was trying to do.

But a minute later, John's dad appeared, standing on the tree facing Nate!

How did that happen?

"John?" His dad stretched his neck to get a better look at his son.

"Dad?"

"What is this place?"

"Jesus is here!"

John's dad looked at him like he was nuts.

Just like he always looked at John.

John got a weird feeling in his stomach. "I have to go."

"Are you serious?" Nate looked at him, wide-eyed. "Your dad is about to change his ways."

"I need to find Jesus."

John's dad stepped off the tree limb.

He walked over the wet sand to John.

Nate turned. He joined John and his dad. "John, just give me a chance," he said. "Let me show you what I can do for you."

John still had that feeling of *wrong* in his belly.

That's when John realized that Nate's voice sounded just like his dad's voice!

"Don't!"

John's father said, "What? I didn't say anything. Don't what?"

John was so confused. Was this really his dad? Or was it an impostor, like the woman at his house?

But through all the questions and confusion, he still held on to the fact that he had to find Jesus.

Nate stepped closer to John.

"John, just come with me, and I promise to make you feel important."

The words tugged at John's heart. He wanted that more than anything. But he felt that he was still watching a magician work.

Jesus.

He hugged me.

He told me I matter.

"Get away from me, Nate!"

The words came out of John's mouth before he had a chance to think about what to say.

"I need Jesus! Not you. Not my dad. I am with Jesus!"

Nate walked away and didn't turn back.

The man who looked like John's dad gazed at him for a second. He shook his head like he was disappointed, and then he turned around and followed Nate.

They left John alone.

The wind picked up.

And blew the dark clouds away.

CHAPTER 10

John kept walking. He didn't know where he was going, but his brain told him that he had to keep moving. He couldn't help but wonder if Nate would come back, or the dragon for that matter.

When he'd gone what felt like miles along the shoreline, John saw the faint outline of a boat. It looked familiar.

From his left, John saw a group of shadow figures move toward the lake.

The dragon's soldiers?

John stopped.

He waited.

The sun was setting.

Evening light was almost gone but still bright enough for him to notice that the men were not covered in black clothes this time. They were all wearing robes.

The disciples!

John ran down the shore toward his new friends.

"You're the boy from the fishing boat?" One of the bearded men stopped.

"Yes! Simon Peter, it's me, John!"

The man greeted John with a big bear hug. It felt good to be cared for.

"Do you want to join us?"

Of course! "Where are you going?" John asked.

Simon Peter pointed across the water. "To Capernaum."

"I'd love to join you."

"Great! Let's go."

John followed the other disciples to the boat. They let him pick his spot, and the men all got in after he was settled. John sat on the right side, near the middle. All he could think about was finding Jesus. That made him think about something else.

"Simon Peter?"

"Yes, John."

"Have you seen a man dressed like me walking around?"

Simon Peter shook his head. "No." The disciple asked the others in the boat, and none of them had seen Nate either.

John wanted to ask if they'd seen the dragon or the snake, but he thought they would think he was nuts.

"Where's Jesus?"

Another man, John couldn't remember his name, said, "He must have been tired after feeding all those people. I just saw Him leave to go be by Himself on the mountain."

John's brain was starting to ache, because if that miracle had just happened, then what about all that time he spent with Nate? How did he do all that and no time had passed?

The same reason you even being here doesn't quite make sense.

John didn't know how things worked here in this *other* world, but he could only imagine that the dragon and his wicked soldiers wouldn't give up trying to attack him. He was exhausted and didn't know how much more of this he could take.

The disciples started to row their boat.

The wind grew like some unseen monster swirling out over the churning water.

Waves slammed against the boat, tossing it back and forth.

John's stomach was going up and down too. He felt

dizzy. The men's voices got louder.

The storm began to rage, and John thought the boat was going to flip over. Like a leaf in the wind, he felt helpless because he couldn't control where he was going.

The fishermen all had fearful looks on their faces.

And then, through the storm, right as it felt as if the boat was about to capsize, John saw a light.

"What's going on?"

"Is it a ghost?"

The light grew.

John thought it took the shape of a man.

"It's Jesus," one of the men yelled.

No way!

John stared hard into the storm. He focused on the light.

It *was* Jesus!

"It is I. Don't be afraid."

The disciples cheered. "Come on. Get in!"

John joined some of the others and helped Jesus get in the boat.

As soon as He was in, the waves and wind died down.

John couldn't believe it.

CHAPTER 11

John was thinking about his dad again. All the times he would come home from the casino in a bad mood never ended well. It was always the same discussion. John hated that he was too afraid to stand up and tell his father to change.

In the Le house, there was never a time to talk. Mr. Le made the rules, and that was that. End of story. John was always being sent to his room when something didn't go the way his dad thought it should have gone.

One night, John had confronted his dad.

"Dad, I want to talk about something."

"What is it now?"

"Well," John said, "I hate seeing you so sad."

"I'm not sad. Why do you think I'm sad?"

John took a deep breath. "My friends at school. . . their parents don't go to the casinos."

"So what? What are you saying?"

"I care about you, Dad. I've been praying that you would be happy again."

"John, you never listen. Going to the casino makes me happy. You need to mind your own business. Now *that* would make me happy."

"Asking Jesus into your heart would make you have real happiness."

His dad looked at John and shook his head in disappointment.

"Son, sometimes I think you're not all there. How many times do I have to tell you that God hasn't been paying our bills. I have!"

"I know I'm only a kid, but the Bible is God's Word, and I get it. He promises to take care of His children."

"Go to your room. I'm done talking to you. Go!"

And John went. But that night something happened that had never happened before. As he went to his room, he heard a smashing sound. Later he found out his dad had thrown his glass against the brick fireplace. John stood in the hallway and heard his dad start to cry. He heard him mumble something about *Can't do it anymore* and *Please save me.*

That was just before John had gone to his sister's

house in New York. Six weeks ago. Who knew what his dad was doing or thinking now.

John's trip down memory lane was interrupted by a beautiful figure of light that made its way down the lakeshore. It looked familiar.

Maybe he was one of the angels who helped save me from the dragon.

The glowing form walked up to him. "John?"

That's when John realized he wasn't in the fishing boat with Jesus and the disciples anymore. "Yes."

"I'm here to help."

"Oh, thank you. Can you help me find Jesus again? I was just with Him in a boat."

"I know. . . ."

"Great!"

"Come on, follow me."

"I'm John. Are you an angel?"

"Hi, John. My name is Antas. I'm. . .just a friend who wants to help."

John followed the man away from the lake. They walked for a long time without saying anything.

When they reached a big hill, Antas stopped.

Despite the warm temperature, a cold wind blew across the land.

John shivered.

Something wasn't right. That's when he realized that Antas hadn't answered his question. John had asked him for help finding Jesus, but the reply was *I know*. The guy never finished his thought.

"I need to go now. I need to find Jesus!"

John looked around and saw that he had been taken into a nightmare. He wasn't standing anywhere close to Jesus. He wasn't near the water but in the middle of a valley filled with not one but six massive dragons, one red and the other five darker than midnight. Crawling around the valley in between the dragons' massive legs were snakes bigger than the anaconda-looking one that had tried to attack John earlier. There were too many of them to count!

And every space of valley floor that was not covered with creatures was occupied by the soldiers who wore black hoodies and black jeans.

Like some demonic orchestra, the hideous gathering of darkness kept their eyes on Antas.

The shape that appeared to be an angel of light yelled out, "Take this child and teach him a lesson!"

The dragons spit angry flames into the sky.

The snakes recoiled, hissing venomous replies.

The dark soldiers began to march in John's direction.

John looked around for a way out but there wasn't any. The one called Antas blocked him from the back.

"I'm sorry, John." Antas started to go dim. "This is where your journey ends."

CHAPTER 12

"Leave. The. Boy. Alone!"

The voice rattled every bone in John's body.

It wasn't scary sounding, but it *was* the most powerful voice John had ever heard.

There was a long pause between each of the four words.

After *Leave*, the dragons rose into the sky and flew away.

After *The*, all the slippery earth crawlers slid far away from John.

Boy pushed back all the hooded soldiers of darkness.

And *Alone* was what the fake angel of light became. At the sound of that powerful voice, all the dark things, big and small, vanished.

And in a flash of light, John was back with Jesus and the disciples!

Jesus was staring at John! "Child, I want to explain why I wanted you to be here when I calmed the storm. It's all about having faith that I am bigger than all of your problems. When your dad says you're not important— that's the storm—remember that I calm you and make everything all right."

John was catching on. "Like when you got in the boat, the storm died down and the water got calm."

Jesus said, "Yes, child."

A man nearby interrupted and asked Jesus a question.

"Rabbi, who sinned, this man or his parents, that he was born blind?"

John looked around and saw that they weren't on water, but back near the temple courts of Jerusalem again. There was a fragile-looking man sitting on the ground in front of them. John tried to recall the Bible story.

Jesus answered the man. "Neither this man nor his parents sinned."

The man who couldn't see held his hands up toward Jesus.

You need to mind your own business.

His dad's voice again.

That's what kids like you should do. Mind your own business.

John tried hard not to think about his dad, but the hurtful words wouldn't leave. They seemed to bring on the dragon earlier, so he kept thinking about being here with Jesus.

"This happened so that the works of God might be displayed in him."

The disciples looked at each other like their Teacher was speaking nonsense. Peter called out, "Surely someone did something wrong to cause this man to lose his sight."

"As long as it is day," Jesus continued, "we must do the works of Him who sent Me. Night is coming, when no one can work. While I am in the world, I am the light of the world."

Son, this whole thing is some sick joke. Just a dream, John. Just a dream. Come on and wake up. The quicker you stop believing in these fairy tales, the sooner you'll grow up and maybe even become a real man. Someone who's worth something.

"Jesus! Help me. Please."

"What is it, child?"

"My dad. I can't stop hearing his ugly words."

"Don't be afraid, John. In Me, you are strong!"

Jesus spit on the ground, made some mud with the

saliva, and put it on the man's eyes.

To the blind man, He said, "Go, wash in the Pool of Siloam."

"John. Child, are you all right?"

John turned around and saw that Peter was the one who asked the question.

"Not really. I don't understand why my dad still gets to me. Even out here with you guys."

"Maybe this can help you understand. That pool called Siloam means *sent*. Watch what happens."

The blind man went into the water and washed the mud away.

Immediately he shouted.

"I can see! I can see! Thank You, Jesus! I can see!"

John's arms were covered in goose bumps. He had just witnessed another miracle! Reading about them in his Bible was one thing, but seeing them happen was something else.

"John?" It was Jesus.

"Yes."

"Are you familiar with how this story ends?"

John thought for a minute. "Yes. The Pharisees question the man and his parents. They don't like what he has to say about You, so they throw him out."

"Yes, and then the man that I gave sight to comes back to Me. He believes in Me as his Savior and worships Me."

John considered all the things that Jesus was telling him.

"I believe in You, Jesus."

"I know, My child. I know. But you don't understand what strong trust is. Yes, you go to church and sing songs. You pray, and I hear every word you speak. I love you, John. Please, hear Me on that."

John was overwhelmed. He remembered another thing his grandmother used to always say. "The book of Isaiah—sixty-first chapter, third verse—says that God will give you a garment of praise instead of a spirit of despair. John, trust God completely that He will always give you His best instead of worrying about things you can't change."

Jesus smiled. "That's right, John. I love your grandmother. She's My precious child, just as you are."

John stared into his Lord's eyes.

"John, every time the clouds move, I move them. When your dad says something to you, I know. I'm there with you. Just like we are right here together. But instead of being afraid and thinking that you don't matter to your dad, I want you to think about how much you matter to Me. Okay?"

John nodded. "Okay, Jesus. Please help me do that."

"I am, and I will."

CHAPTER 13

John felt a chill in the wind, but it felt good. It was a relief from the heat. He wondered how long he was going to be here and how he would ever find his way back home. Was he sleeping back on the airplane? Were people banging on the bathroom door trying to wake him up?

Nothing made sense except Jesus. When John sat with Him or hugged Him or watched Him do something miraculous, everything felt right. On the opposite end of this journey were the times John thought about his dad, and then all the wild stuff started happening. Dragons and snakes. Dark angels.

Exhausted and mentally drained from all the wonders and signs he had witnessed, John needed to rest.

The cave called to him like a powerful lighthouse beam that beckons lost souls in a storm—strong light that reaches through the tempest and shines on the needy.

The cave called to his tired, frightened body and offered rest.

In fact, the cave offered him hope. If he could hide from the crazy creatures and people who had followed him, then surely he would figure out a new plan.

"Lord, if You had been here, my brother would not have died!"

He heard the person's voice—a woman's voice—just as clearly as if she were in the cave.

Why did the words seem familiar?

What Bible story had someone challenging Jesus about their brother dying?

Lazarus?

Was John in the same cave as Lazarus?

If that's really the case, I'm in here with a dead man!

No. No. No!

John ran.

Straight into a wall.

And ran again.

Into another wall.

He tripped over unseen obstacles.

Precious oxygen didn't come easy.

John panicked.

Instead of getting out, John went farther and farther into the darkness.

After what felt like an eternity, he gave up. Trying to escape the nothingness didn't work.

John collapsed onto the damp earth.

The cave had now become his tomb. It wouldn't be long before he too became a part of the void.

God, why couldn't You help me?

Then John heard people talking again. One voice was filled with the sounds of stress and sadness. The other was filled with hope and certainty.

"Lord, the one You love is sick."

"The sickness will not end in death. No, it is for God's glory so that God's Son may be glorified through it."

"Lazarus has been in the tomb for four days! Why didn't You come sooner?"

Many other voices asked Jesus the same question. Even though John was in the cave, he could hear the conversations clearly.

"Lord," a lady said, "if You had been here, my brother would not have died."

Jesus replied, "Your brother will rise again. Where have you laid him?"

John got up and started shuffling his way through the darkness toward the voices.

"Come and see, Lord."

John was blown away. He heard more accusing voices.

"Could not He who opened the eyes of the blind man have kept this man from dying?"

"Take away the stone," Jesus said.

"But, Lord, by this time there is a bad odor, for he has been there four days."

"Did I not tell you that if you believe, you will see the glory of God?"

John was still deep in the cave, but he heard the voices clearly.

"Father," Jesus said, "I thank You that You have heard Me. I knew that You always hear Me, but I said this for the benefit of the people standing here, that they may believe that You sent Me."

John jumped. Right in front of him, he saw the alien thing that had chased him. It changed forms right there in the cave. First, it became the fierce dragon. Then it turned into the shape of the grotesque snake. Next, it changed into the gaunt lion. Then into the man, Nate. Then into the beautiful false angel, Antas.

Finally, the last morph had the alien thing change into a young boy.

The boy stepped closer to John, and John saw himself! The boy looked like his twin.

"Hello, John," the other John said in his own voice. "They call me the Thief."

John was trapped.

But something in his brain clicked on like a light switch.

A memory with Jesus. He had told John that an enemy would attack. . .in many different ways. The boy in front of John was the devil in a bizarre disguise. Just like the dragon, snake, lion, man, and angel. . .they were all insane costumes designed to confuse John. But Jesus had made the truth crystal clear.

Stand up, and with My power you will defeat his plans!

It was time. John trusted Jesus, and that meant he only had one choice. To stand up!

When the Thief was less than two feet away, John kicked his knee. The Thief yelled in pain but managed to shove John back against the cave wall.

John's back exploded in pain, flashing a burst of light in his eyes. He slid down the wall, unable to find the strength to stand. When he hit the ground, he felt a thick tree branch with his right hand.

The Thief came closer, like a wrestler crouching low, ready to attack. John had no time to think. He grabbed the branch and swung it like a baseball bat, connecting with the Thief's other knee. The Thief collapsed on top of John, pinning John's head against the cave floor.

His head brushed against something hard.

John managed to move his arm up and grab the object next to his head. It was a large stone.

He lifted the rock and threw it at the Thief. It hit him in the head, knocking him back, but he was soon on his feet, coming at John again. It was dark, and John saw the staff that the Thief swung at his legs too late. It came hard and fast, knocking John down. His legs were on fire.

John had nothing. There were no more weapons.

No more tricks.

The Thief had finally won.

The powerful words. . . Leave the boy alone.

The same power that raised Jesus from the dead. . .

The lotus flower grows from the darkness.

That was it.

John had to have faith instead of fear. No matter what his eyes saw or his body felt, he had to trust Jesus.

He had to trust that Jesus was more powerful than the Thief.

The power that was pulling Lazarus up from the dead would be the same power that was in John!

Something beautiful had to come from this dark cave.

John used his arms to drag himself across the cave floor. The Thief did the same.

As soon as he got close enough, John reached out and touched the body of Lazarus. "Jesus! You are my Savior!"

John felt the surge of power run through his veins. . . .

The Thief laughed. "Grabbing a dead man? Nice plan. I thought you were smarter than that! Goodbye, John Le."

There was a moment where every sound was silenced. Only the wind that blew through Bethany was heard rustling the leaves on a nearby tree.

"LAZARUS, COME OUT!"

The Thief grabbed John's leg, but instead of smiling in victory, he wailed in horror. A power shoved him off John and slammed him into the cave wall so hard that his body vaporized into a hundred million pieces.

The same power that destroyed the darkness gave strength to John like none other. He was able to stand

and find his way out of the cave behind Lazarus.

The man's hands and feet were still wrapped with strips of linen, and a cloth was still around his face.

Jesus saw His friend and said to the people, "Take off the grave clothes and let him go."

While the crowd celebrated their friend's resurrection, Jesus waved at John and walked over to him.

"Precious child, I need you to know that, in My eyes, you are a miracle too. Please have faith that what I say is true. While you are in the world, the dragon will always be there in the shadows lurking. But he has no power over you, John Le."

He has no power over me.

John closed his eyes and hugged Jesus.

It was the best feeling in the universe.

Real love filled his heart. . .

. . .and it felt so good.

CHAPTER 14

PRESENT DAY

LAS VEGAS, NEVADA

"Come out! We're about to land. You need to get your seat belt on!"

Margaret?

The cave was gone.

Lazarus gone.

Jesus gone.

He was back in the claustrophobic airplane bathroom.

What is happening to me? Where did the Bible land go?

"Come on, John! You have to get buckled!"

He got up and noticed the piece of paper on the floor. He bent down and picked it up. This time he noticed an additional line:

3L3CTUS
John Le
Team Zion, Leader

What on earth was Team Zion? John had never led anything in his life, so this was obviously for another John Le.

"John, you gotta get out of there!"

He folded up the paper and shoved it in his pocket.

He moved the door slider. Red OCCUPIED back to green VACANT.

John expected to see a look of panic on the flight attendant's face, but instead, all he saw was a small, sweet smile.

"Hello, friend, welcome back."

John looked at the woman and wondered how on earth she knew he had been somewhere else.

He shook his head and hurried back to his seat.

What just happened to me?

John found his seat and quickly buckled up.

Minutes later, the plane's wheels touched down.

As they taxied to the gate, John carefully put the picture of the lotus in his backpack. His mom would really love it. When the plane stopped, everybody stood even though it was going to take a while before they could exit.

When it was his turn, John got up and followed the line of passengers down the aisle.

Margaret was waiting for him on the jet bridge.

"Take care, John. Don't forget that you're a miracle to Jesus." She gave him a quick hug before giving a farewell to the passenger behind him.

How did she know?

John concentrated on seeing his mother. She would be a comfort and would ease his nerves. She always knew the right things to say.

As he walked into the terminal, John scanned the crowd, looking for his mother. She was nowhere to be found. He took out his phone and texted her.

She didn't reply.

John kept walking around, thinking maybe she'd gone to the bathroom.

That's when a hand grabbed his shoulder.

John froze.

"Hey, man!"

John turned around and saw his dad standing there.

"Where's Mom?"

"Good to see you too."

Remember Me, John. I'm with you. You are important. I'm proud of you, and I love you very much.

"Where's Mom?"

"I wanted to pick you up. Is that okay?"

John ignored the sarcasm. Things were different now. "Sure. I had an amazing trip."

His dad nodded. "Yeah, your sister called after she dropped you off. Told us all about it."

Even though John wanted to talk about meeting Jesus, he changed the subject. "Can you come to church with us Sunday?"

He waited for the quick deflection. His dad was about to give some reason why he couldn't come.

But surprisingly, none came.

"Let's go home, son."

John followed his dad out of the terminal and through the parking lot. When they got to their car, John slipped into the passenger seat and plopped his backpack on the floor between his feet. He thought about everything he had learned on his Bible journey.

"I want you to come to church, Dad. Jesus loves you."

There it was. John didn't worry what his dad might say. Jesus had told John he was important. John let the words hang there between them as a challenge.

"Son, don't tell me church is going to solve my problems. I've gone to church before and nothing's happened."

John stared out the window.

As they exited the airport, it started to rain.

Don't you worry what happens. Don't worry if your father laughs at you or has some ugly comment.

"I don't know how it all works, but I do know that Jesus is real and that He loves us."

John's father kept his eyes on the wet road and didn't reply.

After a few minutes of silence, his dad spoke. "Where was this Jesus when your mother lost her job? Huh? I know you thought I was a deadbeat dad for going to the casino, but we needed money to pay the bills, and without two incomes, I didn't know what else to do."

"Mom asked you not to."

"I know. But I'm the leader of the family. It's my responsibility to make sure bills get paid."

"Will you come to church and give Jesus a chance?"

More silence.

The rain went from a drizzle to an all-out downpour. John's dad pulled the car off the road into the first parking lot he saw.

Ironically, it was a church parking lot.

Staring at the rain-soaked windshield, John thought about his miraculous adventure. He remembered the dragon and how it pursued him when he took his eyes off Jesus.

His dad let out a big huff. "Son—"

John turned in his seat and faced his father.

"Son, I'm sorry."

This was it. His father was actually going to offer an apology!

"It's okay. I know it must be hard when there's no money."

"No, I'm sorry that I can't give Jesus a chance."

John frowned and turned away from his father and looked out his window again. There was a huge stone cross that had been erected in front of the church. It made him think of his Bible adventure again.

The cross. . .

What Jesus did on the cross for me is the greatest miracle of them all.

And Jesus went to the cross for my dad as much as me and everyone else who believes!

"Dad, we're all broken. Jesus is the only One who can fix us."

At that moment, John's heart for his father turned from anger to sadness. He finally felt sorry for his dad. The only person that could cure him was Jesus.

John kept staring out his window at the cross.

The silence seemed to stretch on for more than minutes. John didn't know what else to say. Finally, he choked out, "The Bible says that if you say *Jesus is Lord* and believe in your heart that God raised Him from the grave, you will be saved."

John managed to turn and face his father.

"Son, please don't waste your time on me."

His father put the car in DRIVE and headed out of the church parking lot.

John felt a sting in his heart. The rain kept coming, and the darkness let it.

"Dad, I know I'm just a kid, but you always told me to stick up for what I really believe in. I'm sticking up for Jesus, and it feels great!"

"John, did you draw a lotus for your mother?"

He had forgotten all about the flower. John bent over and opened his backpack and fished out the unfinished drawing. "Yeah, here. Why?"

No answer. His father navigated the streets of Clark County until they came to their neighborhood.

When they got to their driveway, John's father put the car in Park but left the engine running. He grabbed John by the arm.

"What?" John asked.

"I have to apologize to your mother."

"For what? And why did you ask about the lotus?"

"Your mother and I had a discussion earlier tonight about your grandmother. We talked about how she's always comparing that lotus flower to Jesus. You know, how it grows up from the muddy bottom of a pond and becomes this beautiful creation."

John didn't know where his dad was going with all of this, but he nodded along the way to show he was listening.

"Your mom told me that she knew you were going to draw her a lotus while you were gone. She said that was what you do to remind her that with Jesus, everything will be all right." John's dad grabbed the drawing from him and held it up between them. "Well, I told her I didn't think you would do that. Not because you didn't want to do something nice for your mom. Just because I know how much you love to read, and your sister told us she bought you those Narnia books. I thought the long airplane ride would be the perfect chance for you to read them all."

John saw his mother standing on the porch waving at them.

"You proved me wrong. Now, let's go give this to your mother."

His dad jumped out of the car holding the lotus drawing and ran up on the porch. When he got there, he gave John's mother a huge hug. John got out and joined his parents on the porch. He gave his mother a big hug too.

"I told John I had to tell you I was wrong. Here's what he made for you on the plane." John's dad handed the drawing to his mom.

"Oh, son, it's beautiful."

John smiled. He had to check his disappointment. He was hoping he could have convinced his dad to have faith in Jesus on the ride home from the airport. That would have been perfect. But he knew that Jesus was the One in charge and that things go according to His timing.

The whole Bible journey taught John to have faith, especially when things looked overwhelming and unchangeable. Jesus was big enough to take care of his dad's heart.

"Jesus really loves us, and He is really going to make everything okay."

Holding the lotus flower picture, John's mom led him back in the house. "He sure does, son. And on that note, you have some new friends inside who are really wanting to meet you."

When they got inside, John saw four kids—two boys and two girls—sitting on the couch in their living room.

John's mom pointed to a boy with spiky blond hair. "This is Corey."

"Hi, John. This is Jake, Kai, and Wren. We're the rest of Team Zion. These are our parents." The boy waved at the group of adults standing behind them. "Have a seat, John. I've got something to tell you that's going to blow your mind."

Team Zion? The paper from the airplane.

John sat down. He didn't think anything could top what he had just witnessed with Jesus and all the miracles.

But what came out of the boy's mouth did.

ABOUT THE AUTHOR

Matt Koceich is a husband, father, and public school-teacher. Matt and his family live in Texas.

DON'T MISS THESE EPIC ADVENTURES IN THE IMAGINE SERIES!

Imagine. . .The Great Flood
The last thing ten-year-old Corey remembers (before the world as he knew it disappeared) was the searing pain in his head after falling while chasing his dog, Molly, into the woods. What happens next can't be explained as Corey wakes up and finds himself face-to-face with not one but *two* lions!

Paperback / 978-1-68322-129-6 / $5.99

Imagine. . .The Ten Plagues
The last thing fourth-grader Kai Wells remembers (before the world as she knew it disappeared) is being surrounded by bullies on her walk home from school. What happens next can't be explained as Kai finds herself on the run for her life in ancient Egypt!

Paperback / 978-1-68322-380-1 / $5.99

Imagine. . . The Fall of Jericho
The last thing fifth-grader Jake Henry remembers (before the world as he knew it disappeared) is napping at summer camp. What happens next can't be explained as Jake finds himself surrounded by massive stone walls that rise up all around him—in ancient Jericho!

Paperback / 978-1-68322-714-4 / $5.99

Imagine. . . The Giant's Fall
The last thing fourth-grader Wren Evans remembers (before the world as she knew it disappeared) is getting off the school bus to discover her house engulfed in flames. What happens next can't be explained as Wren finds herself in a beautiful valley with a shepherd named David—in ancient Israel!

Paperback / 978-1-68322-944-5 / $5.99